Adapted by

NANCY PARENT

Illustrated by

HELEN CHEN

Designed by

TONY FEJERAN

☀ A GOLDEN BOOK · NEW YORK

rhcbooks.com

ISBN 978-0-7364-3845-2 (trade) — ISBN 978-0-7364-3846-9 (ebook)

Printed in the United States of America

10 9 8 7 6 5 4 3 2 1

Best friends always stick together! That's what Wreck-It Ralph and Vanellope von Schweetz wanted to do. But when the steering wheel broke on Vanellope's video game, *SUGAR RUSH*, Mr. Litwak had to unplug it. Vanellope and the other racers no longer had a home at Litwak's Family Fun Center.

Ralph and Vanellope wondered if there was any way to FIX IT.

Luckily, there was! Mr. Litwak found a new steering wheel on the Internet. But he couldn't afford it.

So Ralph and Vanellope **BLASTED** into the Internet to get the steering wheel on eBay before *Sugar Rush* was gone forever!

When Ralph and Vanellope landed in the Internet, they were dazzled by the **CHAOTIC** world.

They had to find eBay . . . *but how*?

A cheerful KNOW-IT-ALL named KnowsMore helped them.

At eBay, Ralph and Vanellope started BIDDING wildly on the *Sugar Rush* steering wheel. **They won!**

Sugar Rush Steering Wheel

Seller information:
pjohnston (98★)

Current bid: 27,001.00

00d 00h 03s

POWER UP

But they had **no way** to pay for the wheel.

And with only 24 HOURS to get the money,
things did not look good!

Back in the Internet, the two friends were
BOMBARDED with pop-up ads.

They met Spamley and Gord, who showed
Ralph and Vanellope video games that could
help them earn all the MONEY they needed.

Ralph and Vanellope looked at many different kinds of games. They learned that *SLAUGHTER RACE* paid the most—and Vanellope was born to play it!

This is amazing!

40,000.00

To **WIN**, Vanellope needed to snatch the game's hottest car from its best driver, Shank, and take it to Spamley. Ralph distracted Shank so Vanellope could get the car.

But then Shank drove another car and **BEAT** Vanellope. After Ralph explained to Shank why they needed her car, she decided to help them.

She made a **silly** video of Ralph and told him to take it to a website called BuzzzTube.

BuzzzTube was run by a friend of Shank's named Yesss. She posted the video, and seconds later, Ralph's **inflated cheeks** were all over the Internet!

Yesss said that Ralph could make a lot of money by filming more funny videos.

Soon Ralph and his funny videos became an Internet **SENSATION**!

Yesss sent Vanellope to a popular website called OhMyDisney.com to spread the word.

There, she met **Eeyore** . . .

. . . and **Dumbo**.

Vanellope even made friends with the avatars of the **DISNEY PRINCESSES**.

Thanks to the videos, Ralph made enough money to **buy** the steering wheel!

But Vanellope wasn't thinking about going home anymore. She wanted to go back to *Slaughter Race* with her **new friend** Shank.

If Vanellope went there, Ralph worried that he'd lose his best friend. He told Spamley that *Slaughter Race* was bad for Vanellope.

Spamley took Ralph to **THE DARK NET**. Hackers Double Dan and Little Dan gave Ralph a worm virus that he could attach to the game to slow it down—then Vanellope wouldn't like it anymore. They put the worm in an envelope with a card that said **good luck** and handed it to Ralph.

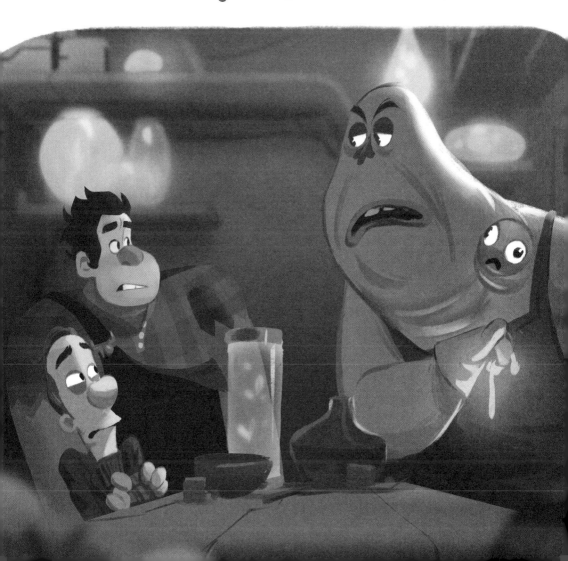

Meanwhile, Vanellope had decided to make *Slaughter Race* her new home. She REVVED up to start her FIRST OFFICIAL RACE. But first she opened Ralph's card and the worm virus fell out.

Ralph and Spamley watched the virus attack
Slaughter Race. The game **GLITCHED**, and a building
COLLAPSED on top of Vanellope's car!

She was knocked **OUT COLD**!

Ralph pulled Vanellope from her car and took her to safety, but he felt awful that she'd been hurt. He admitted to his friend that he'd caused *Slaughter Race* to CRASH.

That upset Vanellope, and she ran away. She never wanted to see Ralph again!

The **VIRUS**, which had grown from Ralph's fear of losing his best friend, was now made up of thousands of Ralph clones. And it had already spread far beyond *Slaughter Race*!

Ralph rushed to find Vanellope, who had gone to see Shank. They had to find a way to DESTROY the virus.

Double Dan and Spamley arrived just in time with a PATCH to eliminate the virus.

But the Ralph clones combined to create a **MONSTROUSLY HUGE RALPH**. It captured Vanellope and grabbed the real Ralph!

"Stop it!" shouted Vanellope. "You're hurting my best friend!" She told Ralph that she would never abandon him. They would **ALWAYS** be friends.

As Ralph's fear of losing his friend began to disappear, so did the **VIRUS**!

With the virus gone, everything went back to normal in the Internet. Ralph and Vanellope were no longer fighting. They even made a **NEW** pact. They didn't always have to stick together. But no matter what, they'd always be **BEST FRIENDS**.